CIRCUS DAY
IN JAPAN

Bilingual English and Japanese Text

Written and illustrated by Eleanor B. Coerr   Translation by Yumi Matsunari

TUTTLE PUBLISHING
Tokyo • Rutland, Vermont • Singapore

Published by Tuttle Publishing, an imprint of Periplus Editions (HK) Ltd., with editorial offices at 364 Innovation Drive, North Clarendon, Vermont 05759 U.S.A. and at 61 Tai Seng Avenue #02-12, Singapore 534167.

Library of Congress Cataloging-in-Publication Data

Coerr, Eleanor.
  Circus day in Japan / written and illustrated by Eleanor B. Coerr ; Japanese translation by Yumi Matsunari. -- 1st bilingual ed.
    p. cm.
  Summary: A Japanese brother and sister take a train from the farm where they live into the city to go to their first circus, where they delight in the jugglers, the trapeze artists, and the big white elephant.
  ISBN 978-4-8053-1059-5 (hardcover)
  [1. Circus--Fiction. 2. Brothers and sisters--Fiction. 3. Japan--Fiction. 4. Japanese language materials--Bilingual.] I. Matsunari, Yumi. II. Title.
  PZ49.31.C65 2010
  [E]--dc22
                    2009041905

ISBN-13: 978-4-8053-1059-5

Distributed by

North America, Latin America & Europe
Tuttle Publishing
364 Innovation Drive
North Clarendon, VT 05759-9436 U.S.A.
Tel: 1 (802) 773-8930
Fax: 1 (802) 773-6993
info@tuttlepublishing.com
www.tuttlepublishing.com

Japan
Tuttle Publishing
Yaekari Building, 3rd Floor
5-4-12 Osaki
Shinagawa-ku
Tokyo 141 0032
Tel: (81) 3 5437-0171
Fax: (81) 3 5437-0755
tuttle-sales@gol.com

Asia Pacific
Berkeley Books Pte. Ltd.
61 Tai Seng Avenue #02-12
Singapore 534167
Tel: (65) 6280-1330
Fax: (65) 6280-6290
inquiries@periplus.com.sg
www.periplus.com

First bilingual edition
14 13 12 11 10   6 5 4 3 2 1

Printed in Malaysia

In Japan near a high mountain and by the blue ocean a little boy was sound asleep. His name was Joji-chan, and he was dreaming about riding on the back of a white elephant.

日本の、あるあおいうみべのよこの、たかい山のちかくで、小さなぼうやがすやすやねていました。ぼうやのなまえは、じょーじちゃん。白いぞうのせなかにのってるゆめをみているところです。

His sister, Koko-chan, was already up and dressed. When she saw Joji-chan still in bed she shouted, "Wake up, sleepy-head! Today we are going to the CIRCUS!"

Joji-chan was awake in a flash and jumped out of bed.

いもうとのここちゃんは、もうおきていて、きがえもすんでいます。じょーじちゃんがまだねどこでねているのを見て、「ねぼすけ！おきなさい！今日は、サーカスに行く日よ！！」とさけびました。

じょーじちゃんは、ぱっと目をさまし、ねどこからとびおきました。

He dressed in such a hurry that he almost put his pants on upside down. Koko-chan helped him fold his bedding and neatly pile it in a cupboard behind the sliding doors.

All the while Joji-chan was thinking about the elephant and wondering if he would see one at the circus.

じょーじちゃんは、いそいできがえます。あわててズボンをさかさまにはくところでした。ここちゃんは、ふとんをきれいにたたんで、おし入れにつんであげました。
「サーカスでぞうさんにあえるかなぁ。」じょーじちゃんは、ずっとかんがえていました。

Since they lived on a farm, the rest of the Shima family had been up for hours. Joji-chan hurried into the kitchen where Mrs. Shima was preparing lunch.

"Mother," he said, "do you think they'll have a big elephant at the circus?"

"Perhaps," said his mother, "but right now you fan the charcoal fire and put water on for tea."

じょーじちゃんのいえのしまいっかは、のうかなので、ほかのみんなはなんじかんもまえからおきています。じょーじちゃんは、だいどころにいって、おべんとうをつくっているおかあさんに言いました。

「おかあさん、サーカスに大きなぞうさんいるかなぁ?」

「いるかもしれないわね。」おかあさんはいいました。「さぁ、いまはすみをおこして、おちゃのおゆをわかしてちょうだい。」

6

Koko-chan went outside where Aunt Sumi-san was hanging wash out to dry on the bamboo pole. Baby sister Miki-chan was sitting in her wicker carriage, playing with the sunshine.

"Today we are going to the CIRCUS!" Koko-chan told her baby sister. "It's too bad you're too young to go, but maybe next year we can all go together."

ここちゃんは、たけざおにせんたくものをほしている、すみおばさんのところへ行きました。いもうとのみきちゃんは、うばぐるまで、ひなたぼっこをしています。
　「きょう、わたしたち、サーカスにいくの！」ここちゃんは、いもうとに言いました。「みきちゃんはまだ小さいから行けなくてかわいそう。でもらいねんはきっとみんなといっしょに行けるわよ。」

"Come along," called Joji-chan, "let's do our chores as fast as we can."

Then Joji-chan began carrying buckets of water from the well to the kitchen. And Koko-chan began throwing grain to the baby chicks. She laughed when she heard them peeping. This is the way they sounded to her: PEEOH! PEEOH! PEEOH!

「さぁ、はやく。」じょーじちゃんはよびました。「早くお手つだいをすませちゃおうよ。」

　そうして、じょーじちゃんは、いどからだいどころへとバケツの水をはこびはじめました。ここちゃんは、ひよこにえさをあげました。ここちゃんは、ひよこのなきごえをきくと、おかしくてわらいました。ここちゃんには、こんなふうにきこえるのです。　ピヨ！　ピヨ！　ピヨ！

Everyone else had already eaten breakfast when Koko-chan and Joji-chan sat down on the cushions to eat theirs.

As Joji-chan picked up his chopsticks he said, "I hope they have the biggest elephant in the world!

"Don't talk," said Koko-chan, and we'll finish our rice faster."

ここちゃんとじょーじちゃんが、やっとざぶとんにすわってあさごはんをたべはじめるころには、ほかのかぞくのみんなはもうたべおわっていました。

じょーじちゃんは、はしをもつと「せかい中でいちばん大きなぞうさんがいたらいいなぁ！」とうれしそう。

するとここちゃんは、「しゃべるとその分、ごはんがおそくなるわよ。」と言いました。

his soup bowl
じょーじちゃんのおわん
joji-chan no owan

his tea cup
じょーじちゃんのゆのみ
joji-chan no yunomi

his rice bowl
じょーじちゃん
のおちゃわん
*joji-chan no
ochawan*

her rice bowl
ここちゃんのお
ちゃわん
*koko-chan no
ochawan*

her soup bowl
ここちゃんのおわん
koko-chan no owan

her tea cup
ここちゃんのゆのみ
koko-chan no yunomi

vegetable dishes
おさら
osara

chopsticks
おはし
ohashi

9

Mrs. Shima had packed their lunch into two thin boxes. "Koko-chan," she said, "you tie them up neatly in my purple bundle-cloth."

"I'll carry the lunch," Joji-chan said, "and Koko-chan can look after the water jug."

"Alright," Mrs. Shima said, "but don't forget to take Daddy's lunch to him on your way."

"We won't forget!" said Koko-chan. "We go right past the rice field anyhow."

おかあさんは、二人のためにおべんとうをつくってくれました。「ここちゃん、おかあさんのむらさきのふろしきでしっかりつつんでちょうだい。」

「ぼくがもっていくよ。ここちゃんは、すいとうをおねがいね。」じょーじちゃんはいいました。

「じゃあね。おとうさんのおべんとう、行くとちゅうわすれないでとどけてね。」

「わすれないわ！どうせ田んぼをとおって行くんだから。」ここちゃんは言いました。

straw slippers
わらのぞうり
wara no zori

best shoes
よそいきのくつ
yosoiki no kutsu

leather slippers
かわのぞうり
kawa no zori

When they were ready, Joji-chan put on his school cap and slid first one foot and then the other into his wooden geta. Koko-chan looked at all her different shoes. "Which ones should I wear?" she asked her brother.

"Don't be silly!" laughed Joji-chan. "The roads are dusty so wear your everyday ones, of course."

用いが出来ると、じょーじちゃんはがくせいぼうをかぶって、木のげたをかた一方ずつはきました。ここちゃんは、いろんなくつを見ながら、「どのくつにしようかな。」とまよっています。
　「ばかだなぁ！土ぼこりの中をあるくんだから、いつものくつでいいにきまってるよ。」

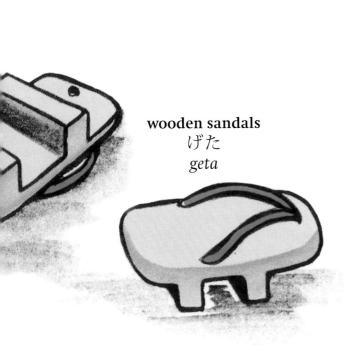

wooden sandals
げた
geta

rain boots
あまぐつ
amagutsu

Girl's wooden clogs
ぽっくり
pokkuri

Off they went down the narrow lane.

"Itterasshai!" called Mrs. Shima. "Watch out for the cars!"

Miki-chan, who was riding on her mother's back, waved with all her might.

"We'll be alright!" shouted Joji-chan and Koko-chan as they waved back.

ふたりは、ほそいみちへと出かけて行きました。

「行ってらっしゃい！」車にきをつけるのよ！

お母さんのせなかにおぶられたみきちゃんも、ふたりに大きく手をふりました。

15

As they hurried along the dirt road their geta went: "KARA KORO, KARA KORO." Joji-chan waved at their good friend, Mr. Scarecrow. Mr. Scarecrow only smiled and said nothing at all.

Mr. Shima was very busy cutting rice in the field. He stopped working only long enough to get lunch from Koko-chan. "Here's ten yen for candy," he said, "and have fun at the circus."

ふたりがじゃりみちをいそいでいくと、げたが　「カラ　コロ、カラ　コロ」
と、おとを立てました。じょーじちゃんは、友だちのかかしさんにも手をふります。
かかしさんは、何も言わずにただわらっています。
　おとうさんは、田んぼのいねかりに大いそがしです。ここちゃんからおべんとう
をもらうと少しやすみました。「ほら、この10円であめ玉でもかいなさい。サーカ
ス、たのしんでおいで。」

Suddenly they shouted: "AH! DENSHA GA KITA!"

"It's the train!" cried Koko-chan. "C'mon, let's run!"

The train station wasn't far, but they ran every bit of the way. Joji-chan was still puffing and panting when he asked at the window for two tickets to Futema, the town where the circus was playing.

「あ！でんしゃがきた！」二人はさけびました。「でんしゃだ！早く、はしるわよ！」
　えきはそんなにとおくはないですが、ふたりはいそいではしって行きます。じょーじちゃんはいきを切らして、サーカスのきているまち、"ふてま"までのきっぷを二まいたのみました。

Inside the train they had a whole seat to themselves. They took turns sitting by the window and waved at every person they saw. Finally the train girl called out: "FOO-TAY- MAH," and they hurried off onto the platform.

でんしゃのせきに、二人ですわると、まどぎわにかわりばんこにすわって、みちゆく人たちに手をふりました。とうとうでんしゃのガールが「ふ〜て〜ま〜」とよびました。二人はあわてて、プラットホームにとびおりました。

Futema Stop was decorated with pretty lanterns and filled with busy people.
"Do you suppose they're all going to the circus?" asked Joji-chan. "If they are," said
Koko-chan, "we'd better hurry and try to get good seats."

ふてまえきは、きれいなちょうちんでかざられて、たくさんの人でにぎわっていました。「この人たちみんなサーカスに行くのかな。」じょーじちゃんは言いました。「もしそうなら、いそいでいいせきをとらなきゃ！」

21

They walked down the main street looking at all the stores.

"Oh good!" said Koko-chan. "There's a candy store!"

They stood looking at all the candy for a long time. There were so many different kinds that it was hard to decide which to buy.

"We can't stay here all day," said Koko-chan. "Let's buy those pink rice cakes."

Joji-chan paid ten yen for the rice cakes and carefully tucked them inside the bundle with their lunch.

大どおりにならぶおみせを見ながらあるいて行くと、ここちゃんが、「やったぁ！おかしやさんだ！」言いました。

　二人はおみせのおかしをながいあいだながめていました。たくさんのおかしがあって、どれにしようかきめられません。

　「ひがくれちゃうよ！」ここちゃんは言いました。「このピンクのおもちにしよう。」

　じょーじちゃんは、10円をはらっておもちをかい、そーっとおべんとうづつみの中に入れました。

Soon they heard the circus music and Koko-chan said, "Oh, let's run! Maybe it has started already!"
They ran very fast, and suddenly poor Koko-chan almost ran right into a ferocious bull. She was so frightened that she hugged tight to Joji-chan.
The bull growled:
"WOOOOOOO!
WOOOOOOOOO!
WOOOOOOOOOOOOOOOOO!"
And Koko-chan covered her eyes with her hands.

するとまもなく、サーカスのおんがくがきこえてきました。「はしろう！もうはじまっちゃったかもしれない！」
　二人は、いそいではしりすぎて、かわいそうに、ここちゃんはもうすこしで、きょうぼうな　とうぎゅうにぶつかるところでした。ここちゃんは、とてもこわくなって、じょーじちゃにしがみつきました。
　　とうぎゅうはうなりごえを上げます。
　　　　「ウ〜〜〜〜〜〜！
　　　　　ウ〜〜〜〜〜〜〜〜！
　　　　　　ウ〜〜〜〜〜〜〜〜〜〜！」
　ここちゃんは、りょう手で目をおおいました。

Joji-chan laughed. "Look," he said, "it isn't a real bull at all!"

"Why, it's only a man!" cried Koko-chan, peeking out between her fingers.

There was another man leading the bull. He was beating a drum: "CHIN CHIN, DON DON! CHIN CHIN, DON DON!"

"Look at the sign on his back," Joji-chan said to his sister. "It says NAKAMURA MEAT STORE IS THE BEST IN TOWN!"

じょーじちゃんは、わらって、「よく見てごらん！本もののうしじゃないよ！」

「なんだ！ただの人かぁ！」ここちゃんは、ゆびのあいだからのぞいて言いました。

もう一人、うしをひいた人がきました。たいこをたたいています。「チンチン、ドンドン！　チンチン、ドンドン！」

「せなかに何かかいてあるよ。」じょーじちゃんはここちゃんに言いました。「なかむらは、この町で一ばんおいしいおにくやさんだって！」

As they crossed a big intersection, Koko-chan watched the policeman directing traffic. "Isn't he graceful?" she said. "When I grow up I'm going to be a policeman like him!"

ふたりが大きなこうさてんをわたったとき、ここちゃんはけいさつかんがこうつうせいりしているのをみました。「あの人はすごいなぁ。おおきくなったら、あんなけいさつかんになりたいなぁ。」

27

People were coming to the circus from all directions.
Some came by bus ....
some came by taxi ....
some by pedicab ....
some by bicycle ....
and small children came by piggyback.
But most were walking, just like Joji-chan
and Koko-chan.

たくさんの人が、いろんなところからサーカスを見にや
ってきました。
あるひとはバスで
ある人はタクシーで
あるひとはじんりきしゃで
あるひとはじてんしゃで
そして小さなこどもたちは、おんぶされて
でもほとんどの人がじょーじちゃん、
ここちゃんのようにあるいてきました。

Joji-chan looked at
the signs and cried,
"There—there's an elephant! And
I bet he's a big white one too!"
"Oh, look," said Koko-chan,
"there's already a ticket line, so
let's hurry."

30

じょーじちゃんは、かんばんを見てさけびました。「ぞうだ！ぞうがいるって！きっと大きくて白いぞうさんにきまってるよ！」
「見てよ。きっぷをかう人がもうこんなにならんでる。いそごう！」ここちゃんは言いました。

Joji-chan bought two tickets. There was a picture of an elephant on them.

They went inside the tent, and Koko-chan's eyes grew bigger and bigger.

"Look up there!" she said. "The tent seems as high as the sky!"

Lots of people were already seated on the raised platform, but Joji-chan saw a place right in the front row.

じょーじちゃんはきっぷを2まいかいました。きっぷにはぞうのえがかいてあります。

テントの中に入ると、ここちゃんの目はまるまると大きくなりました。

「上を見て！このテント、空までとどきそう！」

たくさんの人が、だんになっているせきに、すわっていました。じょーじちゃんは、一ばんまえのせきを見つけました。

They climbed a few steps and took off their geta so they wouldn't dirty the straw mats spread on the platform, because the mats were to sit on. An usher handed Joji-chan a tin pail.

"Here," Joji-chan told his sister, "put your geta in the pail with mine and we won't lose them."

In a moment the stage curtains parted. Koko-chan clapped her hands. "it's starting!" she cried happily. "The circus is starting!"

二人は、かいだんをのぼって、わらのしきものをよごさないように、げたをぬぎました。かかりの人が、じょーじちゃんにかんのバケツをわたしました。

「ほら、この中にぼくのげたといっしょに入れておけば、なくさないよ。」じょーじちゃんは、ここちゃんにいいました。

すると、ステージのカーテンがひらきました。ここちゃんは手をたたいて、「はじまったよ！サーカスがはじまったよ！」とうれしそうに、大ごえでさけびます。

A pretty girl wearing a kimono came onto the stage. She climbed a ladder and started to walk a tightrope. "Look!" cried Koko-chan, "she has geta with red straps just like mine!"

かわいい、きものをきた女の子がステージにたっています。はしごをのぼって、ピンとはったつなの上をあるこうとしています。「みて!あの子のげたのはなおもあかいろ!わたしのといっしょよ!」とさけびます。

The drums rolled as a lady
juggler balanced a screen
on the soles of her feet.
Someone had been hiding on
the other side of the screen
and suddenly PONG!
   A blue bunny came bursting
through the paper.

女の子がしょうじ戸を足のう
らで、バランスをとると、たいこ
がゴロゴロとなりだします。
すると、とつぜん、 ポーン！
　しょうじ戸のむこうがわでか
くれていたのでしょうか、あお
いうさぎさんが、しょうじをや
ぶってジャンプ！

And then there were many wonderful things ...

The man on the flying trapeze ...

And monkeys who loved to tease ...

The seal balancing a ball on his nose ...

And jugglers as neat as you please!

そこからは、たくさんの、すばらしいきょくげいがくりひろげられました。

くうちゅうブランコでそらとぶお兄さん・・・、

やんちゃなおさるさんのきょくげい・・・、

おはなにボールをのせたオットセイ・・・

みごとなジャグリング・・・

The monkey who hung by his tail ...

Another who sat on a pail ...

The seal with a bright parasol ...

And the trapeze artists ...

Oh! Don't let them fall!

しっぽでぶらさがるおさるさん・・・

もういっぴきは、バケツの上にきちんとおすわり・・・

パラソルをもったオットセイ・・・

そして、またくうちゅうブランコ

おっとっと！おっこちそう！！

Next a big red box was put out on the stage. Two dancers came out and danced around the box. They had long white hair that they kept tossing about.

"It's just a box," said Joji-chan. "I wonder what's in it?"

"Maybe there's nothing in it at all," said Koko-chan.

But just at that very moment ...

つぎは、大きなあかいはこがステージにでてきました。2人のかぶきやくしゃが、はこのまわりでおどります。2人は白くてながいかみの毛をぐるぐる回てんさせます。

「ただのはこかな。中になにが入ってるのかな?」

じょーじちゃんがきくと、「なにも入ってないんじゃない?」ここちゃんはこたえました。

すると、そのときです!

39

PONG!!! Out of the box flew a giant Jack-in-the box with a long nose pleated like an accordion!

ポーン！！！ そのはこは、なんと大きな大きなびっくりばこ！アコーディオンのような、なが～いはながついたピエロが出てきました！

They were still laughing at the funny Jack-in-the box when intermission time was announced. Everyone brought out their lunches and started to eat. Joji-chan untied the bundle and got out their lunch boxes. The rice tasted awfully good, and they ate every bit of it.

"Maybe they'll show the elephant soon," said Joji-chan.

"Do you think they'll let us ride on his back?" asked Koko-chan.

"Well," said Joji-chan, "I don't know about little girls, but I'm sure big boys can get on his back." Koko-chan didn't say anything, but she secretly hoped that the elephant would like little girls too.

Suddenly they heard a heavy shuffling noise ... AND ...

二人は、きゅうけいのおしらせのアナウンスがはいっても、あのへんてこなびっくりばこがまだおかしくて、わらっていました。かんきゃくせきのみんなは、おべんとうを出してたべはじめました。じょーじちゃんも、ふろしきからおべんとうだしました。こんなときにたべるおべんとうはなんておいしいのでしょう。二人はひとつぶのこさずたべました。

「もうすぐ、ぞうさんでてくるかな。」じょーじちゃんわくわくしながらいいました。

「せなかにのせてもらえるかな。」とここちゃん。

「う〜ん。でも、小さなおんなの子はどうかなぁ、ぼくみたいな大きいおとこの子ならのせてくれるとおもうけど。」じょーじちゃんがそういうと、ここちゃんは、こころの中で「ぞうさんは、わたしみたいな小さなおんなの子もすきにきまってるわ。」とつぶやきました。

そのときです。とつぜん、大きなあしおとがきこえてきました・・・　そして・・・

A big white elephant clomped in, led by his pretty lady trainer, carrying his trunk high in the air.

Joji-chan was so happy he laughed and clapped all the time the elephant did his tricks.

大きな白いぞうが、かわいいちょうきょうしさんといっしょに、長いはなを上げて、ドシン、ドシンと入ってきました。
　じょーじちゃんは、ぞうさんがげいをするたびに、手をたたいて大よろこびです。

After the white elephant had done many wonderful tricks, the lady trainer asked, "Who is brave enough to ride on the back of this noble elephant?"

Joji-chan and Koko-chan scrambled down from their seats and were the first there. The elephant knelt down, and they climbed on his back. Then the elephant stood up again, and suddenly they found themselves so high in the air that they scarcely dared to breathe. The elephant went walking back and forth in front of all the admiring people, with Joji-chan and Koko-chan ever so proudly on his back.

白いぞうさんの、すばらしいきょくげいのあと、ちょうきょうしの女の子はいいました。「だれか、この大きなぞうさんのせなかにのってみたいという、ゆうきのある子はいますか?」

　じょーじちゃんとここちゃんは、かんきゃくせきからはい出て、いちばん先に出て行きました。そして、ひざまついたぞうさんの上をのぼりました。すると、ぞうさんがまた立ちあがりました。二人はとつぜん高いところに上がったので、びっくりしていきができなるくらいでした。ぞうさんは、じまんげにすわっているじょーじちゃんとここちゃんをのせて、かんきゃくのまえを、行ったりきたりしてみせました。

Soon the circus was over and they started home. Joji-chan talked about the elephant the whole way, but Koko-chan scarcely heard him because she was so busy thinking about the lady tightrope walker.

They got home in time for supper, and at the table Joji-chan told the Shima family all about the elephant. Then Koko-chan had to tell them all about the lady on the tight rope.

まもなくサーカスがおわって、みんないえにかえるじかんです。じょーじちゃんは、かえりみちにずっとぞうさんのことをはなしていました。でも、ここちゃんは、つなわたりのおねえさんのことであたまがいっぱいで、じょーじちゃんの言ってることなどきこえません。

いえにつくと、ばんごはんのじかんでした。じょーじちゃんは、かぞくにぞうのはなしを、ここちゃんは、つなわたりの女の人のことをぜんぶはなしました。

After supper they told their parents goodnight, bowing properly at the doorway, and then they went to bed, to dream about elephants and tightrope walkers.

夕ごはんのあと、二人はお父さんとお母さんにおやすみなさいをいって、ふとんにはいりました。そして、ぞうさんとつなわたりのおねえさんのゆめを見ます。

Koko-chan dreamed she was a tightrope walker wearing the tallest geta in all the wide world!

ここちゃんは、せかい中どこをさがしてもないくらい高いげたをはいた、つなわたりのおねえさんのになったゆめを見ました。

Joji-chan dreamed he was the only trainer in the world who could make an elephant stand on his head!

じょーじちゃんは、ぞうさんの
あたまの上にのることができ
るたった一人のちょうきょうし
になったゆめをみました。

49

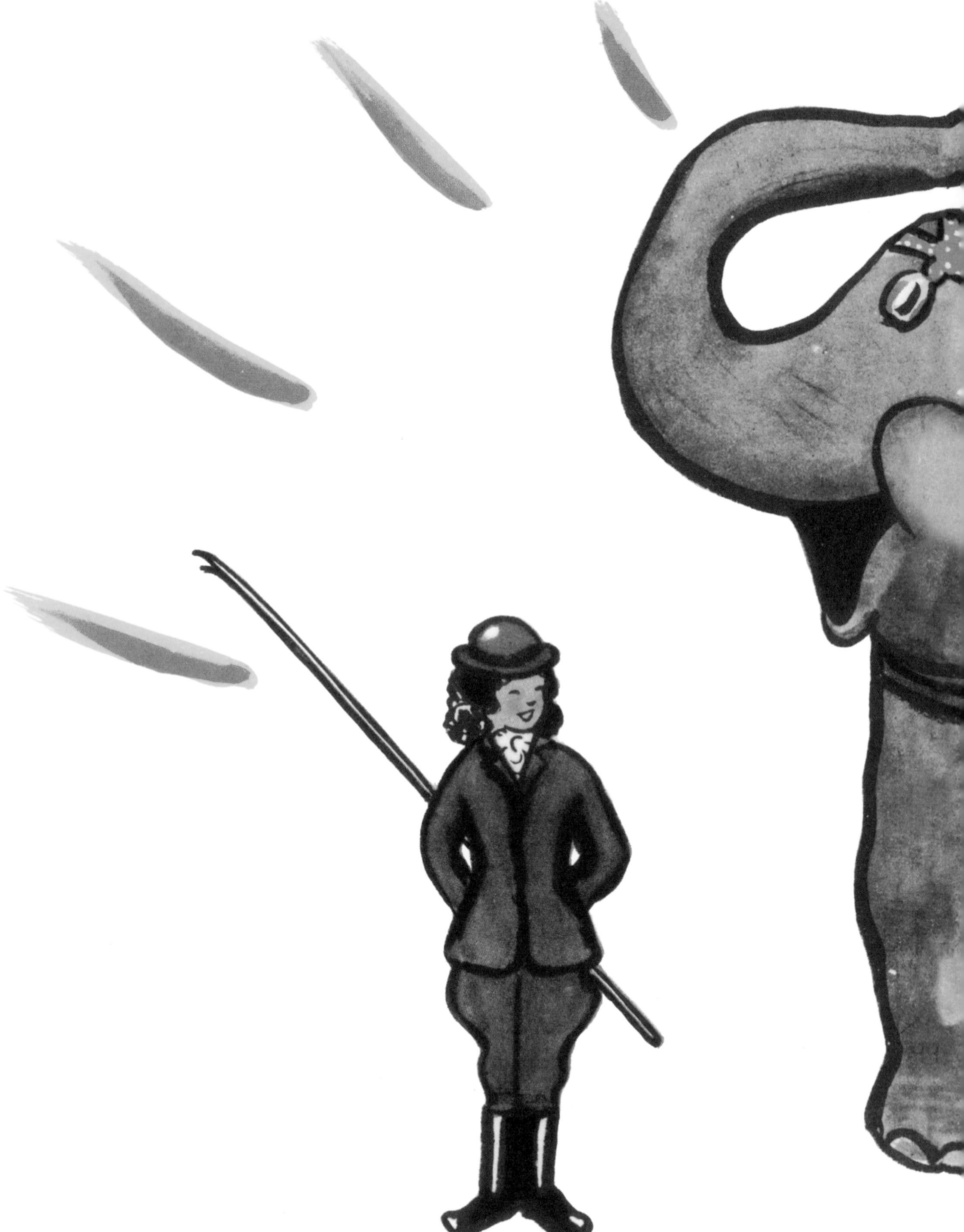